Mary
Had a Little
Lamp

Jack Lechner
illustrated by **Bob Staake**

BLOOMSBURY
CHILDREN'S
BOOKS

Typeset in Bodoni Book
Art created digitally in Adobe Photoshop using nothing more than a mouse,
some imagination, and a reasonable amount of coffee.
Book design by Bob Staake and Donna Mark

Published by Bloomsbury U.S.A. Children's Books
175 Fifth Avenue, New York, NY 10010
Distributed to the trade by Macmillan

Library of Congress Cataloging-in-Publication Data
Lechner, Jack.
Mary had a little lamp / by Jack Lechner ; illustrated by Bob Staake. — 1st U.S. ed.
p.   cm.
Summary: Mary takes her bendy, gooseneck lamp wherever she goes, much to the
dismay of her parents and classmates, but after leaving it at home during summer
camp, Mary finds that she has outgrown her need for her odd companion.
ISBN-13: 978-1-59990-169-5 • ISBN-10: 1-59990-169-2 (hardcover)
ISBN-13: 978-1-59990-192-3 • ISBN-10: 1-59990-192-7 (reinforced bdg.)
[1. Lamps—Fiction. 2. Security (Psychology)—Fiction. 3. Stories in rhyme.]
I. Staake, Bob, ill. II. Title.
PZ8.3.L487Mar 2008   [E]—dc22   2007025069

First U.S. Edition 2008
Printed in Malaysia
(hardcover) 10 9 8 7 6 5 4 3 2 1
(reinforced) 10 9 8 7 6 5 4 3 2 1

For Maude, the light of my life.
                                    —J. L.

For Gillian, who keeps me organized
and (relatively) sane.
                                    —B. S.

Mary had a little lamp—
The bendy, gooseneck kind.
And everywhere that Mary went
She dragged the lamp behind.

She loved to draw a circle
With a pencil round its base.
She loved to feel its metal shade,
So cool against her face.

She loved its quiet company—
It never picked a fight.
She loved its neck, she loved its cord,
And most of all, its light.

She took the lamp to school one day
To teach it how to spell—
But when she tried to plug it in,
The teacher tripped and fell.

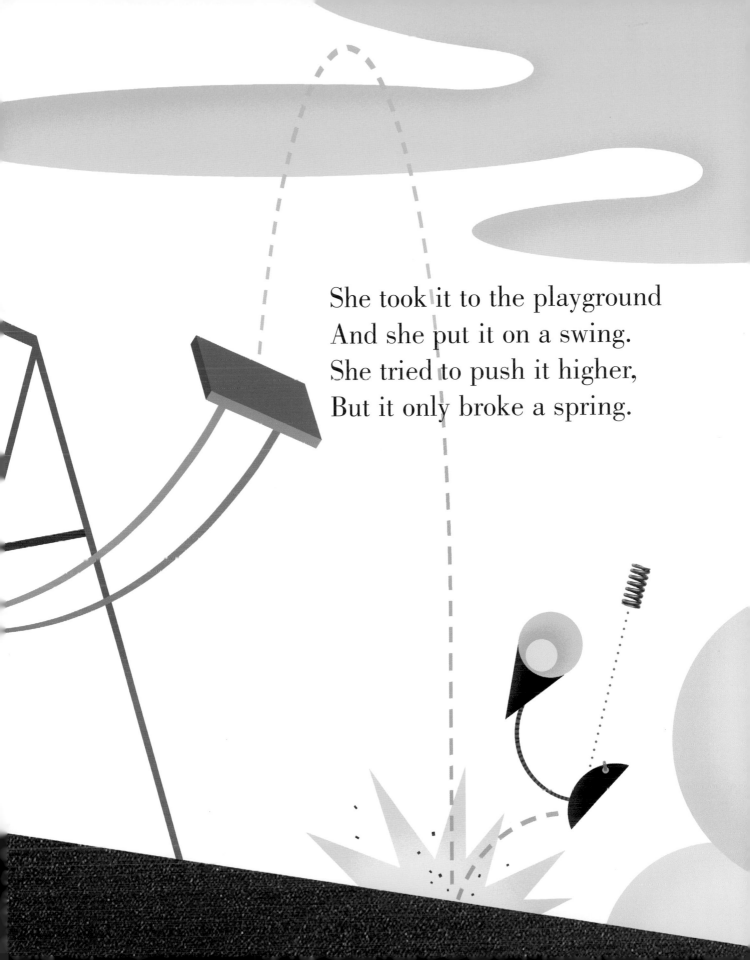

She took it to the playground
And she put it on a swing.
She tried to push it higher,
But it only broke a spring.

"That Mary must be crazy!"
  All the other children cried.
"She really thinks her lamp
  Is gonna make it down the slide!"

"We just don't get it!
Why a lamp?"
Her worried parents said.

"We told her she could
have a dog—
She wanted this instead!"

Their doctor said, "I've never seen
So puzzling a condition.

But lamps are not my specialty—
You need an electrician."

If Mary felt embarrassed,
Then she never let it show.
So everywhere that Mary went,
The lamp was sure to go.

She took it to the movies

And her cousin Debbie's wedding.

She took it out for Chinese food.

She even took it sledding.

She took it to the baseball game,

365

The circus, and the zoo.

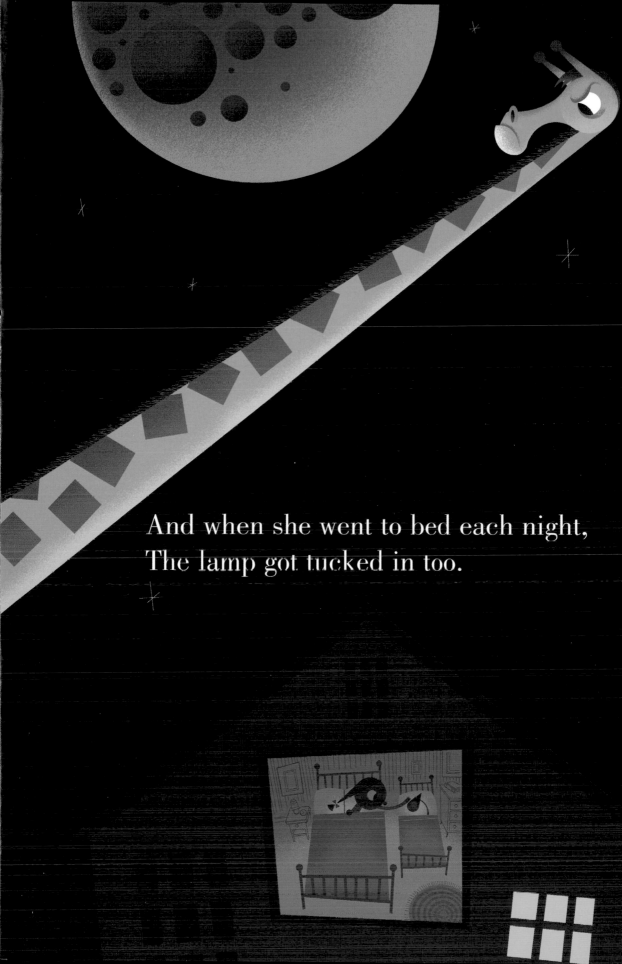

And when she went to bed each night,
The lamp got tucked in too.

But then, one summer, Mary's parents
Sent her off to camp.
And Mary did the strangest thing—
She didn't take her lamp!

She spent the summer swimming
And canoeing, and she found
That she could have a lot of fun
Without the lamp around.

Well, ever since she came back home,
The lamp's been on the shelf,

And Mary's found another way
To occupy herself.

Now Mary doesn't take the lamp
Out sledding on her coaster—
She's much too big for stuff like that!

Now Mary has a toaster.